Holiday House / New York

To my parents, who took me to see real snow,
and to my husband, who gave me my red sled
– J. C.

For Joe, Julie, and Jim
– J. E.

Printed and Bound in March 2012 at Kwong Fat Offset Printing Co., Ltd., Dongguan City, China.
The text typeface is Catseye Medium.
The artwork was created with acrylic paint on paper.
www.holidayhouse.com
First Edition
1 3 5 7 9 10 8 6 4 2

Library of Congress Cataloging-in-Publication Data
Cox, Judy.
Snow day for Mouse / by Judy Cox ; illustrated by Jeffrey Ebbeler. – 1st ed.
p. cm.
Summary: On a snowy day, Mouse is swept outside where he plays in the snow, ice skates on a frozen puddle, and makes sure his friends the birds get something to eat.
ISBN 978-0-8234-2408-5 (hardcover)
[1. Snow–Fiction. 2. Mice–Fiction.] I. Ebbeler, Jeffrey, ill. II. Title.
PZ7.C83835Sn 2012
[E]–dc22
2011007266

Mouse woke up on a chilly morning. He peeked outside. What an icy, lacy, snow-flaky day!

Mexico

Three birds huddled together on the telephone wire. Poor little quivery, shivery birds.

But inside, Mouse was warm and dry. No worries for Mouse!

Down in the kitchen, Mom turned on the radio. Cat rubbed against her legs. Dad went outside to shovel the walk.

"Snow day!" called Mom. "No school."

"Hooray!" yelled the kids. "Let's bake cookies!"

They mixed and baked and frosted and decorated. Then the kids bundled up in their snowsuits and raced outside.

One fat, round gumdrop rolled off the table and bounced higgledy-piggledy into the corner. A treat for Mouse!

Mouse crept across the floor. One step, two steps, silent Mouse. He didn't see Cat, padding and prowling, greeny eyed and greedy. Mouse bent to scoop up his prize. . . . Cat crouched. . . .

Dad came in stomping snow from his boots.

"Not in my clean house!" said Mom.

She grabbed the broom. Snow clumps, Cat, the gumdrop, and Mouse whirled out the door.

THUMP! Mouse landed in a snowdrift. When he climbed out, what a sight met his eyes: Heaps of snow like mounds of mashed potatoes! Flakes of snow like powdered sugar!

The chilly birds fluffed up their feathers and chirped.

"Hello, birds! Have you seen my gumdrop?"

The birds shook their heads.

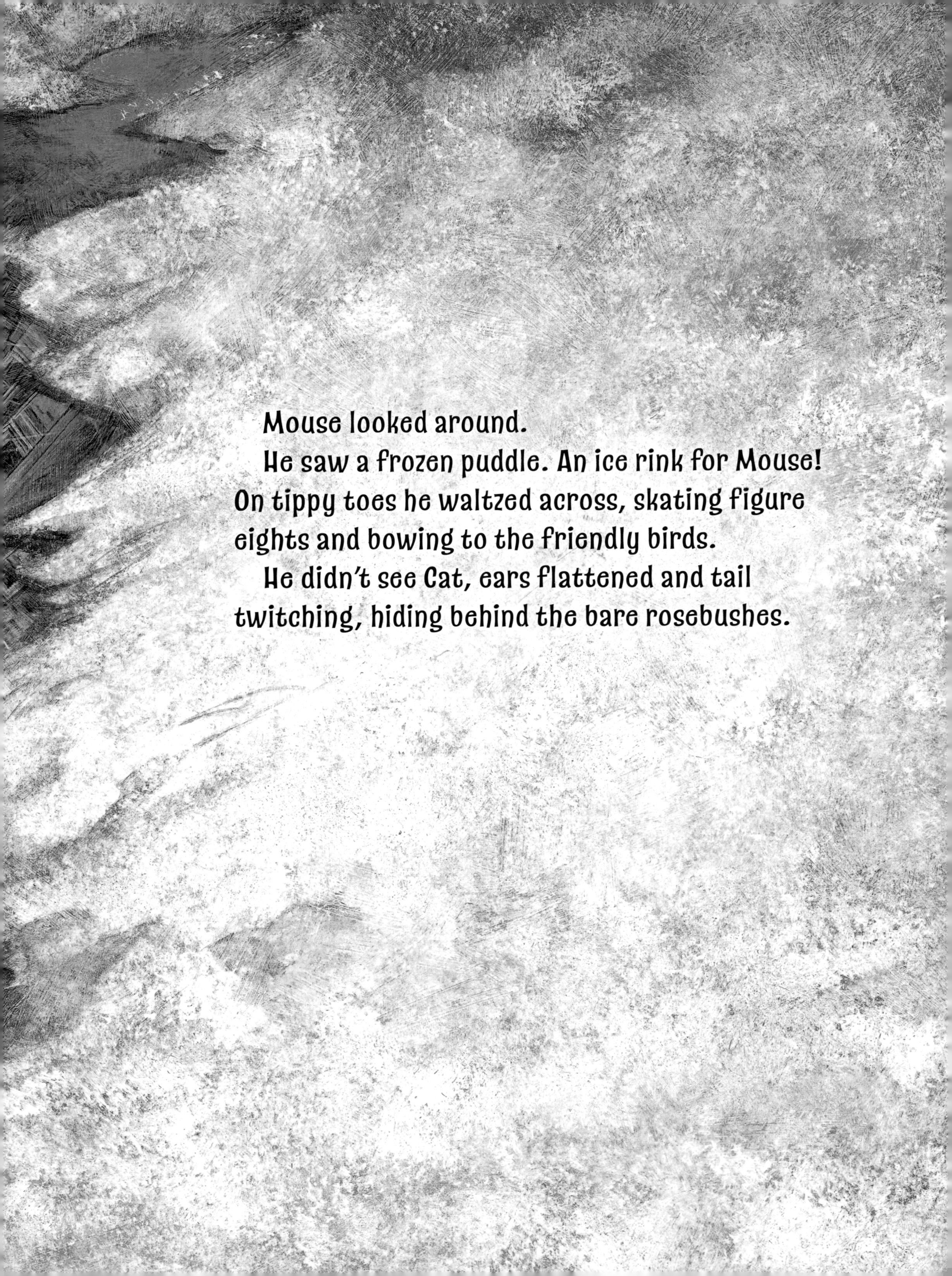

Mouse looked around.

He saw a frozen puddle. An ice rink for Mouse! On tippy toes he waltzed across, skating figure eights and bowing to the friendly birds.

He didn't see Cat, ears flattened and tail twitching, hiding behind the bare rosebushes.

But he did see a mouse-size hill perfect for sledding! He slid down on a curled-leaf toboggan, faster and faster, picking up speed until he landed in a heap at the bottom.

He didn't see Cat, head down and tail up, ready to pounce.

The little birds cheeped, "Watch out, Mouse! Run!"

PLOP! A dollop of snow from the telephone wire dropped on Cat's head. Cat twitched his ears and stalked away, flicking the snow from his paws.

The birds cheered—all clear!

ORANGE

Mouse crept out of the downspout. He rolled snowballs. He made three fat snowbirds and a snowmouse with a berry for a nose. The birds on the wire bobbed their heads.

Now Mouse was cold. His paws were chilly. Tummy empty, time for something sweet or crunchy. Where had that yummy gumdrop gone?

"Hot chocolate!" called Mom. In ran the kids all snowsuited, heavy booted. Mouse scampered between their feet, undetected, unsuspected.

The kitchen smelled cinnamon-spicy. Mouse snacked on crumbs. Soon he was warm and not so icy. But he remembered the quivery, shivery, hungry birds.

The next time the door opened, Mouse was ready. Out in the backyard, Mouse sprinkled his crumbs on the snow. Sharing, caring. “Hungry birds, come get your treat! A gift for my new friends!”

CHARTER BUS
MEXICO
TICKET
BUS STOP

The snow turned pink in the sunset light. The birds chirped their thank-yous. No gumdrop for Mouse, but something better: a warm and toasty feeling deep inside.

Happy Mouse!